W9-BCJ-448

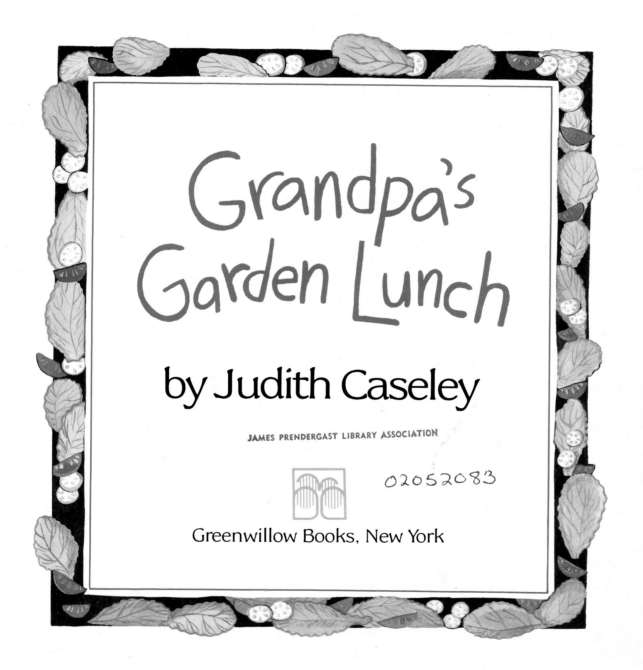

Grandpa's Garden Lunch

by Judith Caseley

JAMES PRENDERGAST LIBRARY ASSOCIATION

02052083

Greenwillow Books, New York

Watercolor paints and colored pencils
were used for the full-color art.
The text type is Bryn Mawr Book.

Copyright © 1990 by Judith Caseley
All rights reserved. No part of this book
may be reproduced or utilized in any form
or by any means, electronic or mechanical,
including photocopying, recording, or by
any information storage and retrieval
system, without permission in writing
from the Publisher, Greenwillow Books,
a division of William Morrow & Company, Inc.,
105 Madison Avenue, New York, NY 10016.

Printed in Singapore by Tien Wah Press
First Edition   10 9 8 7 6 5 4 3 2 1

Library of Congress Cataloging-in-Publication Data
Caseley, Judith.
Grandpa's garden lunch/Judith Caseley.
p.   cm.
Summary: After helping Grandpa in the garden,
Sarah and her grandparents enjoy a lunch made
from home-grown vegetables.
ISBN 0-688-08816-3.   ISBN 0-688-08817-1 (lib. bdg.)
[1. Gardening—Fiction.   2. Vegetables—Fiction.
3. Grandparents—Fiction.]   I. Title.
PZ7.C2677Gr 1990   [E]—dc20   89-23325   CIP
AC

To Suradhuni and Pratibha
and to
Grandpa Lester's garden

${G}$randpa liked to work in his garden.

Sarah liked to help.

Grandpa dug a hole,
and Sarah dropped some seeds
in the ground.
They patted the earth smooth.

Grandpa watered the garden
with a hose.
Sarah used her watering can.

She watered Grandma's herbs.
They were growing in pots,
with their names on sticks.

Grandpa and Sarah watched the birds
in the garden.
Sarah saw a red bird.
"It's a cardinal," said Grandpa.

She saw a blue bird.
"It's a blue jay," said Grandpa.

One morning Grandpa said, "I'll take you to my nursery."
"You're too old for a nursery," said Sarah, laughing.
"It's not for me," said Grandpa. "It's for plants and trees."

Grandpa chose tomato plants.
Sarah chose a plant with yellow flowers.
"It's a marigold," said Grandpa.
"My favorite color," said Sarah.

Grandpa bought some packets of seed
and a dozen yellow seedlings.
"A border for the garden," he said. "Sarah's border."

Sarah dug a hole in the ground.
Grandpa put a plant with yellow flowers
in the hole.

They patted the earth smooth.
Grandpa watered the garden.
Sarah watered Grandma's pots
of herbs, her new border, and
Grandpa's tomato plants, too.

The garden grew and grew.

One day Grandma invited Sarah for lunch.
"What are we having?" asked Sarah.
"We're having the garden for lunch,"
 said Grandpa.
 Sarah laughed.

They went outside to eat in the garden.
On the table was a vase of flowers.
"My border," said Sarah. "How pretty!"
"A garden vase," said Grandpa.

They drank iced tea
with sprigs of mint in it.
"Garden tea," said Grandpa.

They had a lettuce and tomato and cucumber salad.
"Garden salad," said Grandpa.

They ate spaghetti and tomato sauce
with basil in it.
"Garden sauce," said Grandpa.

They had zucchini cake for dessert.
"Garden dessert," said Sarah.
Sarah, Grandma, and Grandpa
finished their garden lunch

and sat out in the sun
by the garden.

JAMES PRENDERGAST LIBRARY

3 1880 0205208 3

E
Caseley, Judith.
    Grandpa's garden lunch

DATE DUE		
FEB 15 1999		

JAMES PRENDERGAST
LIBRARY ASSOCIATION
JAMESTOWN, NEW YORK
Member Of
Chautauqua-Cattaraugus Library System

2/91